WNBA SUPERSTARS

A'JA WILSON

by Tracy Abell

FOCUS READERS®
NAVIGATOR

WWW.FOCUSREADERS.COM

Focus Readers is distributed by North Star Editions:
sales@northstareditions.com | 888-417-0195

Produced for Focus Readers by Red Line Editorial.

Photographs ©: Rich von Biberstein/Icon Sportswire/AP Images, cover, 1; Phelan M. Ebenhack/AP Images, 4–5, 6, 9, 26; Janet Blackmon Morgan/The Sun News/AP Images, 10–11; Hannah Foslien/AP Images, 13; Rainier Ehrhardt/AP Images, 15; James Crisp/AP Images, 16–17; Tony Gutierrez/AP Images, 19; Rick Havner/AP Images, 21; Jevone Moore/Cal Sport Media/AP Images, 22–23; Thurman James/Cal Sport Media/Zuma Wire/AP Images, 24; Eric Gay/AP Images, 28

Library of Congress Cataloging-in-Publication Data
Names: Abell, Tracy, author.
Title: A'ja Wilson / by Tracy Abell.
Description: Lake Elmo, MN : Focus Readers, [2022] | Series: WNBA Superstars | Includes index. | Audience: Grades 4-6
Identifiers: LCCN 2021040534 (print) | LCCN 2021040535 (ebook) | ISBN 9781637390733 (Hardcover) | ISBN 9781637391273 (Paperback) | ISBN 9781637391815 (ebook) | ISBN 9781637392294 (PDF)
Subjects: LCSH: Wilson, A'ja, 1996---Juvenile literature. | African American women basketball players--United States--Biography--Juvenile literature. | Women basketball players--United States--Biography--Juvenile literature. | South Carolina Gamecocks (Basketball team)--Juvenile literature. | Basketball for women--United States--Juvenile literature. | Women's National Basketball Association--Juvenile literature.
Classification: LCC GV884.W588 A44 2022 (print) | LCC GV884.W588 (ebook) | DDC 796.323092 [B]--dc23
LC record available at https://lccn.loc.gov/2021040534
LC ebook record available at https://lccn.loc.gov/2021040535

Printed in the United States of America
Mankato, MN
012022

ABOUT THE AUTHOR

Tracy Abell lives in the Rocky Mountain foothills, where she spent many, many hours in gymnasiums watching her son play basketball. His dedication to the game inspired her to head out to their backyard hoop, where she'd shoot 100 free throws. Tracy's FT percentage hovered around 71 percent.

TABLE OF CONTENTS

WNBA

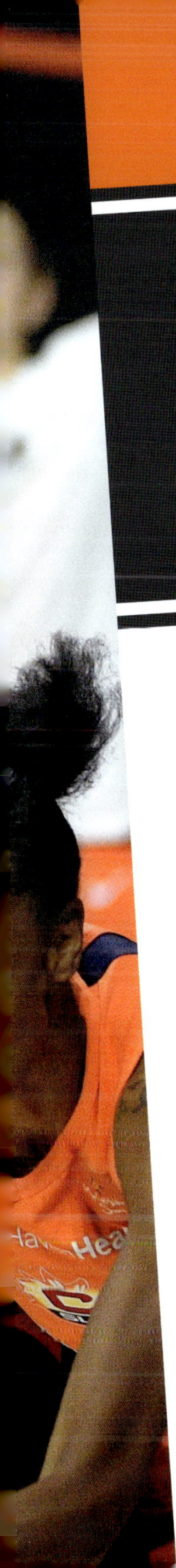

CHAPTER 1

GAME 5 ON FIRE

The Las Vegas Aces were facing the Connecticut Sun in the 2020 Women's National Basketball Association (WNBA) playoffs. It was Game 5 of the series. The winner would move on to the Finals.

In the first quarter, A'ja Wilson of the Aces battled for position on an inbound pass. She was guarded closely by two Sun

A'ja Wilson of the Las Vegas Aces grabs a rebound during Game 5 of the 2020 WNBA semifinals against the Connecticut Sun.

Wilson attempts a shot during Game 5 of the 2020 WNBA semifinals.

players. One defender rotated off Wilson. The other stayed glued to Wilson's back. When Wilson got the ball, the defender bumped her. But Wilson spun off and nailed a jumper.

Wilson proved why she had been the regular season's Most Valuable Player (MVP). She crashed the boards for rebounds. And she outworked the defense to get open shots. Still, the Aces trailed by six at halftime.

The game tightened during the third quarter. The teams traded the lead throughout. Wilson kept the pressure on. Halfway through the third, Sun center Brionna Jones drove for a layup. But Wilson smacked the ball away. Wilson's teammate gained possession and scored. That put the Aces only one point behind.

A minute later, the Sun turned over the ball again. Wilson cruised downcourt for an easy layup. She was on fire.

Wilson pushed even harder during the fourth quarter. She got the ball at the three-point line and easily drove through the defense for a layup. The Sun players looked tired. Wilson was tired, too. She'd played every minute of the game. But she rallied to score the last nine points for her team.

Even so, Game 5 went down to the wire. With less than two seconds on the clock, the Sun's DeWanna Bonner attempted a three-pointer to tie the game. She missed. The Aces beat the Sun 66–63.

Wilson was the game's high scorer with 23 points. Eleven of those came in the fourth quarter. In fact, Wilson scored more points in the fourth than the whole Connecticut team. She also

Wilson puts up a jumper during Game 5 of the 2020 WNBA semifinals.

recorded three blocks, four **assists**, and 11 rebounds. Game 5 was Wilson's third straight **double-double**.

Unfortunately for Aces fans, the team lost to the Seattle Storm in the Finals. But Wilson's Game 5 performance had proved she was a superstar.

22
21

CHAPTER 2

SOUTH CAROLINA STAR

A'ja Wilson was born on August 8, 1996, in Hopkins, South Carolina. Her father, Roscoe, had played professional basketball in Europe. But when A'ja started playing basketball at age 11, she didn't even want to play. Her dad was the coach, and she sat on the bench a lot. Roscoe trained A'ja so hard that she got

A'ja Wilson moves to the basket during a high school game between Heathwood Hall and Dreher.

mad. But A'ja decided she wanted to be great. She kept training.

By high school, A'ja was a leader on the court. Her teammates valued her attitude. Even with a broken wrist, A'ja went to practices and did the sprint drills. She also became a star. In her senior

THE VEST

A'ja's dad wanted her to get stronger and be ready for opposing defenses. So, when other kids left the gym, A'ja kept practicing. She shot layups with and rebounded a 5-pound (2.3-kg) ball while wearing a 20-pound (9.1-kg) vest. A'ja sometimes wanted to cry when she saw that vest. But when her game got better, she realized those drills really did help.

In 2014–15, Wilson was the only college freshman to rank in the top 20 in both scoring and rebounds.

year, A'ja scored 37 points and led her team to an **overtime** victory in the state championship. By that point, she was the No. 1 college **recruit** in the United States.

Wilson stayed close to home. She went to the University of South Carolina.

The school's basketball coach, Dawn Staley, knew Wilson was under a lot of pressure. So, Staley didn't start Wilson during her **freshman** year.

Wilson didn't get mad about playing off the bench. She trusted her coach. And the strategy worked. The Gamecocks won their first Southeastern Conference (SEC) championship. Wilson was named the 2015 SEC Freshman of the Year.

By her second year, Wilson understood her role better. Before, she hadn't cared if opponents scored on her. But now, she started working hard on defense. That effort paid off. Wilson was named the 2016 SEC Defensive Player of the

Wilson drives against a Jacksonville defender during the 2016 NCAA tournament.

Year. Plus, the Gamecocks made it to the National Collegiate Athletic Association (NCAA) tournament both years. However, that still wasn't good enough for Wilson. She wanted to win the NCAA championship.

SOUTH CAROLINA
22

CHAPTER 3

COLLEGE CHAMPION

A'ja Wilson's 2016–17 season started strong. In a practice game, Wilson and teammate Alaina Coates combined for 38 points. The Gamecocks kept it up all season. They earned a No. 1 seed in the NCAA tournament. However, Coates got hurt and couldn't play. Wilson's leadership skills went into high gear.

A'ja Wilson puts up a shot during a 2017 NCAA game against Kentucky.

Wilson proved to be a big-game player. During the semifinals, the Gamecocks trailed Stanford by nine at the half. Wilson's defense kicked in. She blocked two shots and grabbed eight rebounds. The Gamecocks led by four at the start of the fourth quarter and won the game. Wilson recorded a double-double.

The NCAA championship brought out Wilson's best. South Carolina led most of the game against Mississippi State. But in the fourth, Mississippi State got within four points. Wilson sparked the Gamecocks when she blocked a shot. Seconds later, she sank a jumper. Then she made a layup, and the Gamecocks

During the 2017 NCAA tournament, Wilson averaged 19.2 points per game.

were ahead by 10. With under three minutes left, Wilson blocked another shot. After that, she scored the next four points. Thanks in large part to Wilson, the Gamecocks won their first national title.

In Wilson's final year, several of the championship players were gone. Wilson set a new goal to be a great teammate.

She taught her younger teammates it was okay to make mistakes. She also showed them how to work together. Wilson led the Gamecocks to the Elite Eight that season. Once her college career was over, Wilson headed for the WNBA.

GRANDMA HATTIE'S PEARLS

Few people were more important to Wilson than her grandmother, Hattie. The two talked about everything. Hattie gave a 13-year-old A'ja her first pearl necklace. Wilson has worn pearls ever since. Hattie passed away in 2016 at age 95. After that, Wilson thought about quitting basketball. But she played on, believing Hattie was always close. On senior night, fans received imitation pearl necklaces in honor of Wilson and Hattie.

DAWN STALEY

When Dawn Staley finished college in 1992, the WNBA didn't exist. So, she played pro ball in Europe and played for Team USA. Staley won three Olympic gold medals. She joined the WNBA in 1999.

Between WNBA seasons, Staley was a college coach. In 2008, she began coaching at South Carolina. She coached A'ja Wilson for Wilson's entire college career. In 2021, Staley and Wilson teamed up again. Wilson played for Team USA at the Olympics. Staley was the team's head coach. The two helped Team USA win the gold medal.

Dawn Staley made the WNBA All-Star team five times.

ACES
22

CHAPTER 4

NO. 1 ACE

The Las Vegas Aces selected A'ja Wilson with the No. 1 pick in the 2018 WNBA **draft**. In Wilson's first pro game, the Connecticut Sun's defense double-teamed her. Sometimes they even triple-teamed her. Wilson handled the pressure. She recorded a double-double. She also had two assists and two blocks.

A'ja Wilson drives against Nneka Ogwumike of the Los Angeles Sparks during a 2018 WNBA game.

Wilson faces a double-team in the paint during a 2019 game against the Connecticut Sun.

One month later, Wilson played another incredible game. This one came against the Indiana Fever. Wilson came out hot, scoring 10 points in her first five shot attempts. The game ended up going into overtime. With two minutes left, Wilson drove to the basket and scored. She drew a foul and went to the free-throw line. She missed but scored again seconds later. The Aces won 101–92. Wilson had scored 35 points and grabbed 13 rebounds.

At the end of her first season, Wilson was named WNBA **Rookie** of the Year. She was also picked for the All-Star team. Even so, the Aces struggled and didn't make the playoffs.

SUPPORTING OTHERS

Wilson started the A'ja Wilson Foundation during her rookie year. She wanted to help children dealing with **dyslexia** and bullying. Wilson had also struggled with dyslexia and bullying as a kid. She'd received support and had been able to overcome those challenges. Wilson wanted to support other kids so they could achieve their dreams, too.

Wilson attempts to block a shot during a 2020 game against the Dallas Wings.

At the start of the next season, Wilson averaged 15 points per game. Then she got hurt and missed a month. But Wilson scored big in her first game back. She and center Liz Cambage led the Aces to a huge win. The Aces made the 2019 playoffs. They advanced to the semifinals but lost to the Washington Mystics.

In 2020, many WNBA players focused on more than just basketball. They also spoke out about social justice. They supported the Black Lives Matter movement. Wilson wrote a "Dear Black Girls" essay. She shared her experiences of **racism** as a Black girl and as a Black woman. Wilson wanted Black girls to know they weren't alone. She was rooting for them.

On the court, the Aces had lost two starters to injury and health problems. Wilson just worked harder. She led the team all the way to the Finals. Even though they lost, the 24-year-old Wilson was voted the 2020 WNBA MVP. During a

At the 2021 Olympics, Wilson led Team USA to win its 50th straight Olympic game.

very difficult year, Wilson had been a role model on and off the court.

In early 2021, the University of South Carolina revealed a new statue of Wilson. Black girls grinned as they got their pictures taken next to Wilson. The statue was a reminder that anything was possible. After all, superstar Wilson had started out hating basketball.

A'JA WILSON

- Height: 6 feet 4 inches (193 cm)
- Weight: 195 pounds (88 kg)
- Birth date: August 8, 1996
- Birthplace: Hopkins, South Carolina
- High school: Heathwood Hall Episcopal School (Columbia, South Carolina)
- College: University of South Carolina (Columbia, South Carolina) (2014–2018)
- Pro team: Las Vegas Aces (2018–)
- Major awards: WNBA Rookie of the Year (2018); WNBA All-Star (2018–2019, 2021); WNBA MVP (2020); Olympic gold medal (2021)

FOCUS ON
A'JA WILSON

Write your answers on a separate piece of paper.

1. Write one sentence that describes the main idea of Chapter 3.
2. Would you want to work as hard at basketball as A'ja Wilson did growing up? Why or why not?
3. What year was Wilson named the MVP of the WNBA?
   - **A.** 2016
   - **B.** 2018
   - **C.** 2020
4. How did practicing with a heavy vest help Wilson get stronger?
   - **A.** Playing with added weight built muscles.
   - **B.** Playing with added weight was more fun.
   - **C.** Playing with added weight made it easier to move fast.

Answer key on page 32.

GLOSSARY

assists

Passes that lead directly to a teammate scoring.

double-double

A game in which a player has double-digit numbers in two categories.

draft

A system that allows teams to acquire new players coming into a league.

dyslexia

A condition that makes it hard to read or write letters and to recognize words.

freshman

A first-year student.

overtime

An extra period to determine a winner in a tie game.

racism

Hatred or mistreatment of people because of their skin color or ethnicity.

recruit

An athlete whom college teams are interested in.

rookie

A professional athlete in his or her first year.

TO LEARN MORE

BOOKS

Buckey, A. W. *Women in Basketball.* Lake Elmo, MN: Focus Readers, 2020.

Hoehn, Jim. *WNBA*. Minneapolis: Abdo Publishing, 2021.

Omoth, Tyler. *The WNBA Finals.* North Mankato, MN: Capstone Press, 2020.

NOTE TO EDUCATORS

Visit **www.focusreaders.com** to find lesson plans, activities, links, and other resources related to this title.

INDEX

Answer Key: 1. Answers will vary; **2.** Answers will vary; **3.** C; **4.** A